# The Toad Hunt

by JANET CHENERY
Pictures by Ben Shecter

A Science I CAN READ Book

HARPER & ROW, PUBLISHERS ○ New York, Evanston, and London

*To my mother and father*

Teddy and his father

were in the vegetable garden.

They were pulling up weeds.

Teddy reached for a weed,

and something jumped!

Teddy jumped too.

"Wow!" he said.

"Frog, you scared me!"

Teddy's father

looked at the lump

that jumped.

Its skin was brown and bumpy.

"That's not a frog,"

his father said.

"That's a toad."

"It looks like a frog,"

said Teddy.

He squatted

and gave a hop

to see if he could jump

like a frog.

"How do you know it's a toad?"

he asked.

"A toad looks fatter than a frog,
and its skin is lumpy,"
said his father.
"Frogs have smooth skin
and they live near water.
Toads live in gardens
or in meadows,
or ponds,
or anywhere
there are insects."

"Will I get warts if I touch him?"
asked Teddy.

"Peter says he got his wart
from a toad."

"I don't think so," said his father,
"but we can ask Dr. Barlow."

Teddy looked at the toad.

It had warts all over it!

When they got back to their house,

Teddy telephoned Dr. Barlow.

"Hello, Dr. Barlow," he said.

"Do toads give you warts?"

"No," said Dr. Barlow.

"Have you got a toad

or a wart?"

"I don't have either," said Teddy,

"but I saw a toad.

Will it give me a wart?"

"No," said Dr. Barlow.

"It won't give you anything.

How do you know it's a toad

and not a frog?"

11

"Because we found it in the garden,"
Teddy said, "and it had lumpy skin."

"Oh," said the doctor.

"It certainly sounds like a toad.

Did it give a little jump

or a big one?"

"A big one," Teddy said.

"That sounds like a frog,"

said Dr. Barlow.

Teddy tried to remember.

Was it a big jump?

Was it a little jump?

"I'll have to look again,"

he said. "Thank you, Dr. Barlow."

The next afternoon

Teddy and Peter went to the garden

to look for the toad.

They looked around the tomatoes,

near the beans,

in the carrots and radishes,

and under the pea vines,

but they could not find

the toad anywhere.

Teddy remembered

what his father had said.

"Toads like to live

where there are lots of insects,"

Teddy said.

"How about the pond, then?"

said Peter. "There are plenty there.

I got bitten by a mosquito once."

"I got stung by a bee," said Teddy.

"Okay, let's look there," said Peter.

So off they went

down the lane to Polliwog Pond.

As they came through the tall grass

near the pond,

they heard a splash.

The water rippled

in half circles.

"It's a toad!" Teddy cried.

"Not if toads are fat and lumpy

and make little jumps," said Peter.

"This one was long and skinny,

and it jumped a mile."

A tiny head appeared

in the middle of the pond.

It was brown and green.

Its skin was smooth, not warty.

"I guess that *is* a frog,"

sighed Teddy.

"Let's be quiet," he whispered,

"and maybe he'll come out."

They got on their hands and knees.

They crawled around the pond.

But the brown and green head

gave a *Glonk!* and disappeared.

Teddy tried to hop

like a toad.

Peter made great jumps

like a frog.

Suddenly Peter stopped.

He was eye to eye

with a turtle.

"A yellow and black one!"

Teddy shouted. "That's a good turtle!"

"Will he bite?" Peter asked.

"Let's see," Teddy said.

He took a piece of grass

and tickled the turtle's nose.

The turtle pulled its head

under its shell.

Peter and Teddy watched it.

The turtle stuck its head out a little.

It looked at a grasshopper

twitching on a daisy.

In a flash

the turtle's head shot all the way out,

and the grasshopper was gone.

"I think it bites," Peter said.

"Let's go find your toad."

Teddy sat on a big rock

at the edge of the pond.

Peter looked carefully in the grass.

Then he lay on his stomach

and looked into the water.

"You watch the pond," said Teddy,

"and I'll watch everywhere else."

He turned his head slowly

from side to side.

"No toads here," said Peter,

"just little fish and polliwogs.

Wait!" he cried.

"There's something funny!"

"What?" Teddy asked.

"Come and look," Peter whispered.

Teddy crept up to Peter.

They looked into the water.

"A salamander!" Teddy said.

"With red spots," Peter added.

"Oh, boy, a red-spotted salamander,"
said Teddy.

"Watch him. He's eating water bugs,"
Peter said.

They watched the salamander
dart about under the water.
It ate three water bugs
and chased a polliwog.

"Are polliwogs baby fish?" Peter asked.

"No," said Teddy, "they're baby frogs."

"What are tadpoles, then?"
Peter asked.

"I don't know," Teddy admitted.

"Let's ask your father,"
said Peter.

As they were leaving
they heard a quick swish
in the tall weeds.

They looked carefully,

but all they could see

was a little ripple.

The grass moved as if a small breeze

was blowing through it.

At dinner Teddy told his father,

"Peter and I looked and looked

for that toad,

in the garden,

down the lane,

and even around the pond,

but we couldn't find him anywhere."

"No toads at Polliwog Pond?"

asked Teddy's mother.

"I thought lots were there."

"No," said Teddy. "Those are all frogs.

They don't have warts.

They. have smooth skin.

They don't hop like toads.

They make flying jumps into the pond."

"You know a lot

about frogs and toads,"

Teddy's mother exclaimed.

"Yes," said Teddy, "but I can't find

that toad we saw in the garden.

Peter and I saw a frog

and a red-spotted salamander

and a black-and-yellow turtle

that ate a grasshopper,

and we heard a swish in the grass—

I think it was a snake—

but no toad."

"Perhaps another one
will turn up tomorrow,"
said Teddy's father.
"But now it's time for bed,"
said his mother. "Hop along."

"Okay," said Teddy, but he didn't hop.

He moved very slowly

on his hands and knees.

First one foot,

then a hand,

then the other foot,

then the other hand.

"Hurry up, Teddy," his mother said.

"I can't hurry. I'm a turtle,"

Teddy said very slowly.

"We'd better find that toad,"

said Teddy's father,

"so you can hop again."

Teddy finally got upstairs.

When he took his bath,

he became a salamander.

36

He darted about in the tub.

The soap was a water bug,

but it didn't taste very good.

His mother kissed him good-night.

His father told him a story

about a frog

who really was a prince.

Teddy fell asleep

and dreamed about his toad.

The next morning

Teddy's mother said,

"Let's have a picnic tonight,

down by the pond."

"Fine," said Teddy's father.

"Can Peter come too?"

Teddy asked.

"Certainly," said his mother.

That evening they all walked
down the lane to the pond.
Teddy's father
carried the picnic basket.
His mother carried sweaters
and a pair of binoculars
to look at birds.

Teddy carried the thermos jug

full of lemonade.

Peter carried a long stick

to toast marshmallows

and to ward off turtles.

They sat down

near the edge of the pond.

Teddy's father opened the basket.

He gave everyone a hard-boiled egg.

Teddy's mother looked

through the binoculars

at a bird that was singing

in an elm tree.

"It's a hermit thrush," she said.

She handed the binoculars

to Teddy's father.

"Can you tell what bird it is

by hearing it sing?" Peter asked.

"Yes," said Teddy's mother.

"Each kind of bird has its special song.

When you get to know them,

their songs sound as different

as a cat's meow

and a dog's bark."

"How about a frog and a toad?"
Teddy asked.

"Do they sound different too?"

"Yes," said his father.

"Each kind of frog and each kind of toad
has its special croak.

If you get to be a frog and toad expert,
you can tell them apart too."

Peter and Teddy listened

to the distant song of the thrush.

"Mother knows a lot about birds,"

Teddy said.

"Your father knows a lot about toads,"

Peter added.

"Sandwiches, anyone?"
asked Teddy's father,
and they all ate
chicken and cucumber sandwiches.

"Let's feed the polliwogs," said Peter.

He took a crumb from his sandwich

and dropped it into the water.

The crumb sank slowly,

almost to the bottom.

A little fish swam up

and caught it.

"What are tadpoles?"

Teddy asked his father.

"They are the same as polliwogs,"

his father said.

"You mean they are baby frogs?"

Peter asked.

"They are either baby frogs

or baby toads," Teddy's father said.

"*Poll* is an old word for head.

*Tad* is an old word for toad.

So a tadpole is a toad head."

"Can you guess what *polliwog* comes from?" he asked.

"*Poll* means head," said Peter.

"Does *wog* mean frog?"

"No," said Teddy's father.

"It's from another old word meaning wiggle."

"A head-wiggle!" shouted Teddy.

He jiggled his head

back and forth at Peter.

56

Peter tucked *his* head
in and out of his shirt,
like a turtle.

"Bananas and cookies for dessert,"
said Teddy's mother.

A frog croaked in the reeds
on the other side of the pond.

"That frog can have my banana,
but I'd like a cookie," said Peter.

Another frog croaked near the first one.

Teddy took the binoculars

and tried to find the frogs.

A third croak, longer and higher,

sounded close by.

Teddy looked at the ground

through the glasses,

trying to find that frog too.

"I see a huge ant

crawling up a tree trunk,

and a moth as big as a bird,

and a thistle

as big as a haystack, but—"

The croak sounded again,

almost like a trill.

"*There* he is!" Teddy cried.

"What a fat frog!" he said.

"Let me see," said Peter.

He looked through the binoculars.

"That's not a frog, Teddy," he cried.

"That's a toad!"

"A toad?" Teddy said.

They all went over to see it.

It gave three quick little hops.

"That certainly is a toad,"

said Teddy's father.

"Yes," Teddy sighed.

"That certainly is some toad!"